Praise for *The Left Parenthesis*

"Round and moving, nourished by the author's identifiable style and a fascinating management of allegorical and fantastic elements. A world. Or, rather, a whole universe, that of the writer, polysemous and suggestive."
—**Xavi Aliaga,** *El Temps*

"Poetic and allegorical. A very special atmosphere."
—**Anna Guitart, Tria 33**

"A short novel of intense chill, of letting go with each sentence, of refined writing and with a universe that contains pain and doubts, with the overwhelming fantasy of the rawest reality."
—**Esteve Plantada,** *NacióDigital*

"I started on a Sunday in the early afternoon and had already finished it in the evening. I couldn't get up from the couch. The rhythm of her prose caught me completely and surely it would have taken me less to finish it if it weren't for the fact that every two or three pages I had to stop and reread the excerpt to savor it again. You know what I'm talking about, right? When you feel completely identified with a story and know that the reflections you are reading will serve you at one time or another and you need to emphasize them. The protagonist talks about maturity, relationships, and self-discovery. Reflections that are interspersed with a disturbing, visceral, and poetic story."
—**Elisenda Solsona**

THE
LEFT PARENTHESIS

Muriel Villanueva

Translated from the Catalan by
Megan Berkobien & María Cristina Hall

Illustrations by Aitana Corrasco

OPEN LETTER
LITERARY TRANSLATIONS FROM THE UNIVERSITY OF ROCHESTER

Originally published in Catalan as *El parèntesi esquerre* by Males Herbes

Copyright © 2016 by Muriel Villanueva

Translation copyright © 2022 by Megan Berkobien and María Cristina Hall

Illustration copyright © Aitana Corrasco

First Open Letter edition, 2022

Library of Congress Cataloging-in-Publication Data: Available.

ISBN Paperback: 978-1-948830-52-2

Ebook ISBN: 978-1-948830-51-5

This project is supported in part by an award from the National Endowment for the Arts and the New York State Council on the Arts with the support of the Governor of New York State and the New York State Legislature.

The translation of this work has been supported by the Institut Ramon Llull.

LLLL institut ramon llull

Printed on acid-free paper in the United States of America

Cover Design by Alban Fischer

Interior Design by Anuj Mathur

Open Letter is the University of Rochester's nonprofit, literary translation press:

Dewey Hall 1-219, Box 278968, Rochester NY 14627

www.openletterbooks.org

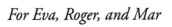

For Eva, Roger, and Mar

After one writing class a student, in amazement, said, "Oh, I get it! Writing is a visual art!" Yes, and it's a kinesthetic, visceral art too. I've told fourth-graders that my writing hand could knock out Muhammad Ali. They believed me because they know it is true. Sixth-graders are older and more skeptical. I've had to prove it to them by putting my fist through their long gray lockers.

Natalie Goldberg,
Writing Down the Bones

I plant my left foot on the station platform, bring the heels of my sneakers together, and the train door beeps behind me. My eyes closed, I wait. I breathe in the slope of pines in front of me; to my back, a fog of cables, to my back, the small station refinished in white and beige paint. The train takes off, I turn my body one hundred eighty degrees and, right past the other platform, I see a brilliant sea and a white sail unhurriedly cutting through it. I'm traveling in old jeans and a nursing shirt the color of faded sea. Against my breasts now heavy with milk, inside an ergonomic carrier, a baby—my child—sleeps with her face to me. I'm thirty-eight and a widow.

You were dressed in white, from head to toe. Today I want to strengthen my aura, you said. You were wearing white, wide-legged pants and, beneath your white, button-down shirt, a white undershirt on inside out. And I didn't mention that your shirt was on wrong because I'd started working on that not-mothering-you thing.

We weren't living together any longer. You had moved to another apartment in the same part of the city for a while. We said, It'll be a few days or weeks and will help us take our gears apart and start over.

We were traveling by train, with our daughter, to someplace a bit farther north: to Casetes Beach. You were radiating light and I no longer wore my wedding ring. The afternoon before, while we were walking on the beach a way down from our place, I'd glanced at your hands. What's wrong?, you asked. I just wanted to know if you still wear your wedding ring. Always, you replied. Always.

I walk through a white-tiled, slightly futuristic tunnel beneath the station, the tunnel that'll lead me to town, a town with only three streets. Three streets, three hundred residents, two coves, a hotel, a public-access beach for water sports, and thirty-three *casetes* running along the waning crescent of the larger cove, just shy of a quarter mile long. Everything cradled by pine-covered mountains. Everything surrounded by a silence broken only by the train. A few descending steps mark the tunnel's birth, and it dies as the shiny metal handrails and gray-tiled stars give way to a winding staircase that leads even farther down. Or the other way around.

Staircases to two separate worlds.

Going back would be an uphill battle.

I grab hold of a rolling Hello Kitty backpack filled with cloth diapers, a stuffed Nemo, a few changes of clothing, my white laptop, and a wireless mouse.

Senyora Lali—I'm guessing—waits for me on a wooden bench between the two flights of winding stairs I come upon at the end of the tunnel. As soon as she sees me, she rushes over and cries:

"Honey, let me help you with your suitcase!"

I stop and let myself be cared for. When we're closer, she wipes both her hands on her greasy apron then holds out the right one to say hello.

"I'm Lali. Muriel, right?"

I nod and when she glances at my daughter, she softens her voice:

"Ah, what a sweet little thing . . ." She strokes my daughter's freckled cheek with the delicate, princess-like touch of a finger, then lifts that same finger to her old lips, gesturing for me to hush.

"Follow me, *nena*," she whispers.

We descend the second set of winding stairs, cross the asphalt street, and walk down a few last steps—this time going straight down.

Now I'm here. One foot already in the sand. The sand I craved. Casetes Beach.

"You can get to our place from the next street over, right behind there, but I'll take you through the beach so you can get your bearings, and because, honey, it's just so beautiful."

Cloaked in white and pine green, the thirty-three *casetes*—that's what the cottages are called here—are perched on columns, raising them nearly five feet off the sand. Lali careens as she carries the suitcase in the air but won't let me help her. We push onward, more than halfway up the beach, toward the hotel that draws the northern cove to a close.

"It's this one. Lovely, right?"

Lovely, and quite so. Everything white, an open terrace with a green baluster for a roof, unlike the usual triangle shape, and a large, sliding glass door divided into three white segments out front. You get in by way of a cement staircase that climbs right-ward toward the rear street and stops, halfway up, in front of a green, wooden door that screeches and tells of saltpeter and fish. We go up. Lali sets the suitcase on the ground.

"It's just that we never use it anymore. You can't imagine how happy I am that someone will get joy out of it."

She tugs on the cords of the green, wooden blinds and draws back the white curtains, letting in the scorching sun.

"When Aineta told me one of her professors was looking for a *caseta* to write in, well, I was just *so* excited. I'll leave your key here," she says, setting it inside the entryway table drawer. "We won't bug you at all. I've let everyone know. My grandfather built this place almost a century ago but, in a way, it belongs to all of us now, though the Barcelona side of the family keeps their distance and the rest of us small-town folks come here in our bathing suits straight from home. I'm sure you get it."

You can tell Lali had just spruced the place up.

The cabin amounts to two rooms separated by a wall and joined together by an archway: a dining room with a small kitchen attached, a room with a double bed, a tiny, corner bathroom, and a spiral staircase leading out to the terrace.

"I wrote down my address for you," she says, reaching into her apron pocket. "My address and a little map." She leaves a scrap of paper on the floral oilcloth covering the table. "I have a washing machine at my place. Don't be silly and go cleaning anything by hand, alright? Especially with the baby and all. You promise?"

I promise with a nod and smile. She doesn't yet know that I'm your typical hippie who refuses to buy disposable diapers.

She exits like a soft wind after showing me what she's left in the fridge for my first day and letting me know I'll have to take care of my future meals. She leaves behind a sweet scent, the muted sound of espadrilles, and, burned into my retinas, the memory of her badly colored red-orange hair—roots showing.

I told you as soon as we'd laid eyes on the *casetes*, remember? I told you one of my novels would take place here. You laughed. Don't you feel like writing down the things that might happen here? You shook your head and I said, Of course, if there were a dead dog around then it'd be right up your alley, but that cove, seen from this angle . . . That's your kind of thing, you replied, It'd fit right into a novel of yours, that's for sure.

The three of us had lunch near the southernmost part of the cove, next to some rocks in front of a restaurant, on a beige, cement bench behind two white beach showers whose tops were painted sky blue. I no longer had to say, Don't eat more than your half. We took photos. The line of *casetes* smiled at the still, Mediterranean waters and our daughter, who wasn't even eight months old, had known how to smile at the camera for a while now. She was eating her cauliflower with venturing hands. We were all wearing sandals and I thought you needed to trim your nails but didn't say anything. Little by little, the mama-me and the insolent-boy-you machine of ours had finally run out of batteries— whether this was only seemingly true terrified me as much as if it were real.

The house is mine for twenty-one days. Twenty-one days for me and my daughter alone. I look down and she's still sleeping in her carrier, against my breast. I take out the bright little pink hat with white flowers that my husband bought to protect her from the sun. She lets out a soft trill and moves her head slightly. I touch her curls, still fine and still short; she doesn't have all that many yet. She opens her eyes and rolls her tiny black pupils upward to look at me, her dense and curving eyelashes flutter. When she knows it's me, she smiles and shows me her six new teeth. In twenty-one days the second nine months will have ended and exterogestation will be over.

I reach my hand behind my back, click the baby carrier open, and lift the baby out, my hands beneath her armpits. I set the carrier down on the red chair and we edge toward the center pane of the patio door, which I open wide. Mar rubs her eyes at the brightness of the water a few feet ahead. A teenage couple lies out on the sand, kissing. There, where the seawater's tongue laps at the shore, a starfish naps and soaks.

I'm not sure what I'm doing here.

I said I was coming here to write and now I don't want to.

Have I even said anything interesting in these first few pages?

I've come to say goodbye, to scatter his remains, sure, and now I remember: his ashes are in my suitcase, too. I'm sorry I didn't write that down before. Maybe I didn't know it yet.

And there's a photo: him in the foreground, dressed in white with his shirt on inside-out, sitting in front of Bar dels Pescadors, right around the corner from here.

It was a month or so ago, the day we found Casetes Beach—you had just started your first novel:

A dog warned the main character, a beggar, that his best friend, another beggar, had died. After following the dog, the boy would find his friend's body, lifeless and with his organs missing, inside a dumpster. The boy's mission—his external conflict, as you'd say—was to bury him.

That same evening, we sharpened our pencils on all the little details of that nameless beggar's internal conflict as we made our way back home, where you no longer lived.

Every day, the sun wakes us up. We sleep close to one another in our double bed and Mar breastfeeds. "It's an all-you-can-eat buffet," as a friend from back home would say. I sleep naked and she sleeps in nothing but her cloth diaper and amber necklace. The sun breaks through the salty horizon, slips in through the windows out front—I haven't touched the curtains since Lali first drew them open—then crosses the arch of the half-wall and hits our eyelids, under which we dream of him. We dream about his out-of-tune songs and his shameless dancing, about his long, dirty fingernails as well as his nails when trimmed and polished. When I open my eyes, Mar has hers already locked on mine, a huge grin on her face. She stretches and lets out little groans that don't mean anything yet. I envy her.

On Sunday, Aina brought over a bouncer and a highchair for the baby, two essential tools for mothers of infants who still can't crawl. I put Mar in the highchair while I clean myself up a bit, throw something on, make a light breakfast, and wash diapers by hand as the sun rises, distancing itself from the sea as if outwitting gravity. Two hours of her little shouts, nibbling hands, pecking at cornflakes, and playing on the table with a big handful of shells that we collected together.

Then she gets sleepy again and, with her in my lap, while she sucks and snores softly, I sit at the table with my laptop to write this piece of shit.

Up until then there was the child-you and the adult-you. One being dismantled and the other taking shape. And you couldn't tell them apart. After Mar's birth they went from not being so fond of one another to not being able to stand each other at all. They'd elbow each other to get ahead. They'd chew one another out and then do the same to me. When I'd speak, I didn't know which one I was scolding, which one I feared, or which one was scarier. I'd yearn for them both. Then there was the your-mother-me, mother-of-an-infant-me, and your-wife-me, each of us trying to find time to write or swim or meditate or do yoga, all three of us in one big embrace, forming a small circle, looking inward, molded into a thick ball of arms, hands, long necks, and twisted legs. Deaf, blind, grasping onto a smaller, reddish-orange ball of flowing lava— the remains of child-me, forever an orphan.

Then I remember what my father had said twenty years before, at a portside bar, a phrase that was his to my mind but that I would later read in the works of the greats: "Don't speak unless you can improve upon silence."

I don't want to leave Casetes Beach.

Casetes Beach, with its waning-moon shape, is a metaphor for my belly, now shrinking with the end of exterogestation. Lali's white and green *caseta*, where I'm staying now, is my heart, and it goes bum-bum, bum-bum. The other thirty-two *casetes* make up my diaphragm and, at least for now, they're not moving at all. I don't want to leave this place. I wash the clothes and diapers by hand and stretch them out on the little rooftop terrace, where everything soaks up the scent of the sea and gets sticky with saltpeter, but we're steeped in it, too, so there's no use in trying to avoid it.

I don't want to leave this place, but we're out of food.

I text Aina, but she says she's not here during the week, so she sends me her WiFi password and suggests I sit out on her front steps, since the signal's better there. I throw on my wide-legged red pants and a mustard T-shirt. I put my baby in her carrier, tuck my laptop under my arm, and go. I leave the beach for the first time in three days. Three boys—who look about twelve years old—stay behind, playing ball as an excuse to show off who can jump the highest. I take the stairs. A train goes by and doesn't stop.

I wish I had the hair I've been dreaming of for years: long—very long—and wavy, with visible grays. It just skims my shoulders now, but even a breeze can get it messy and tangled without even trying. Right now, I want my hair tangled in knots. Very, very tangled. At night, I like to use Lali's tortoiseshell comb—a few of her red-orange hairs with white roots still snagged in the teeth—and have it get caught in the mess so that I have to give up before planting one last kiss on Mar's ripe cheek and switching off the golden table-lamp with its haughty modernist airs.

For the first time since I got to this town, I walk down its three streets, which I only remember from that first day when we visited, with my already sick-and-dying husband.

I sit on the stone steps at Aina's house, which was easy to spot—"blue and yellow with an arched door," she wrote—and start typing. Fettered to me, Mar starts licking my cleavage. I undo two buttons, take my breast out, lower the carrier to my waist, and push my boob up with one hand. Then my baby girl locks her lips on me. I put in a little online order at the biggest supermarket in the region's capital.

I knew you weren't well, but I pretended it wasn't true, because the whole thing made me sick, too. If you died, so did I. If we were a pair, what would that make me afterward?

We took the train from town, which was a little farther south but also along the shore. You wore all white, I dressed like confetti, and Mar was as playful as ever. You held our baby girl on your lap, and I took pictures of you as we talked about the beachfront apartment we'd buy once our finances improved. I was convinced that, as soon as I stepped off the train, I'd find my place in the world, just a little farther north from where we'd planned to settle down. But no.

The minute I got off the train, I knew I could never live here.

Still, Casetes Beach stole my heart. Not the organ, but the feeling.

I came to get it back so I could run away right after. The sun is setting when Mar wakes up from her afternoon nap and I, wearing nothing but my underwear for hours now, close my laptop. I put her in the highchair, we play with shells, eat home-made applesauce. I hide under the table and suddenly reappear, like her father used to do, and her laughter traces dimples on her cheeks. Her orange T-shirt, which I've already washed twice since we've been here because I only packed three, says: *C'est moi la plus belle.* She's got my husband's eyes: black, immense, and asymmetrical. With open palms, she strikes the table hard, so hard.

What are we doing here?, I suddenly think.

My daughter looks straight at me. She's guessed that I'm not all there.

What have we lost?

My heart, my voice, the memory of his figure that spring day . . . I don't know. Who was he? Who did I marry? Why did he leave that way? No. I can't really say he abandoned me without warning. I often think it was me—that I'm the one who beat him to death. I was unrefined, true, but also persevering and precise.

I pull a black shirt over my milk-stained nursing bra and throw on a filthy pair of pants. Barefoot, I pick up the baby and use Lali's oversized, white scarf to fasten her to my body. I lock the door, go down eight steps, and we're on the sand.

I beeline away from the *caseta* until I touch the sea, which seems sleepy today, with the tip of my toes. The water reminds me of who I am. Its coolness rouses and envelopes me, molding to my shape. It says, "I'm here. Are you?" I feel all that with only one foot in, ankle-deep. My jeans are slightly wet, but it's hot out, so I don't care.

I walk slowly until my right big toe hits against . . . the starfish I saw my first day here, from the window. I crouch down to peer at it and could swear it's moving, breathing, alive. Mar juts her arm out from the white scarf and smiles, pointing her finger. I stand back up before she can touch it.

From behind the simple hotel that rounds off the beach's north side—the light turquoise one that's been *cerrado-closed*, since last fall, up until a few days ago—an anemic rhythm scuttles my way. I start tracing the shore with my steps as Mar claps her hands.

I didn't come here because he died.

I came because I died. Or I came to die.

Slowly, I realize I'm hearing tinny music coming from a cell phone. From the sand, I walk up the cement ramp that joins the beach to a small esplanade behind the hotel. Three trees cast their shade on two showers and a few cement and wooden benches lined up in rows, their backs facing each other. Two young guys with shaved heads sit on one of the benches and smoke hash, facing the second, smaller cove. I remember seeing them here with some girls, that first day we came.

It's been five years since I smoked cigarettes, ten

since I smoked pot, and twenty since I smoked *that*. I look at Mar, asking her permission, and go up to them.

We've done this separating-for-a-while thing twice. I always thought stories should carve out "The End" before ever having to get to that.

The first time was five years ago. We were at the city center and you forgot an empty Bic pen on the shelf. After that time, I ended up throwing out lots of full ones over the years, since they'd end up in the wash, where they'd explode inside your pockets.

The second time—this time—was two months ago, in the beach apartment that's still our home. You forgot your hatless Playmobil cowboy on the shelf. A little plastic sign at his horse's feet read *wanted*. I found the black hat under the furniture a few days later—the cats were playing with it.

I fell in love with you because, when you came to my writing classes, you said that a pen with no ink was a metaphor for death. You were eighteen and I was thirty-two.

You liked Westerns because you needed examples of masculinity that were different from the ones you saw off-screen, right?

The day you left my home for the first time, when we lived in the city, was the day you started dying, I guess.

The day you left our home for the second, most recent time, when we lived farther south, it was as if you had wanted to say, I'm a man and I don't need toys or cowboys or dicks, and that's that.

I superglued that black plastic cowboy hat onto the picture I took of you here at Bar dels Pescadors, because when I took it, you were no longer the same.

I bit my tongue right after taking that picture. I was eating potato chips straight from the bag, remember? I didn't eat for days, it hurt so bad.

The two young guys with buzz cuts look at each other, but end up passing the pipe. Smoking hash while gazing out at the sea, closing my eyes before I let out the smoke—that's all I wanted. Just once. I turn my head so as not to get the stink all over Mar, and they laugh.

"Again, Miss. Don't worry, we've got more."

But I shake my head no and smile thankfully, handing it back. Instead of leaving them, I lean my back against one of the showers—a cement column painted white and sky blue, like the ones at the other end of the beach. The cell phone keeps playing that shitty music and I'm happy we're on the same page, speaking Catalan. One is Asian and the other one is Black.

"What are you doing in town?" the Black guy

says, staring at my bare feet. "Are you staying in a *caseta*?"

I nod, and the other one asks, "All alone? With the baby?"

And it all comes back. That typical fear, the one men give me. I peel my back from the shower and pull my shoulders back. At just sixteen or seventeen, these kids spark the fear of men in me—which my husband never did. Men, capable of.

The masculine collective in my head: divided in two. Men, capable of. Boys, needing. Fearing. Scaring. Receiving. Giving. A husband fourteen years younger than me. I'm a widow and I'm scared. Scared shitless.

"Don't leave, Miss. We've got rum and coke. Just a little?"

And I leave, take the ramp down to the sand, and shake my dizzy head no, no, no.

We weren't fucking anymore, so. No, you didn't like when I talked that way. We weren't making love anymore. Sometimes I'd tell you I needed a man to make love with, a real man. Then we'd be dogged by the abuse I carried around with me, an unrooted and volatile abuse that I'd never managed to fully make out and that always filled my head when you were inside of me. And then giving birth, obstetric violence, the bitch forcing down the medicine, the fucking gynecologist with a face like the rabbit from *Alice in Wonderland*, the forceps, the fucking scar. The physical scar that would sound out the muted pain of an entire life of a girl playing a grown-up. It stung. When it stopped stinging it was already too late. By then a sea had formed between us, two bare islands amid an ocean of cloth diapers, breast milk, and the rusty mechanisms of a clock.

How could you have died like this?

I just can't.

Your ashes are on the nightstand, inside that sterile-looking jar, but you know that already.

Giving up your young body, the fleshy tips of your thin fingers. Giving up your hunger for me, breastfeeding you.

A car horn wakes us up as it echoes through the cove behind the *casetes*. Then the engine turns off, I hear a door open and close, and some knuckles rap against my bedroom window, which opens out to the street. I look at the golden, '70s-style alarm clock on the nightstand: 10:10 A.M. already. Mar stretches out—hands high up, feet far down—and laughs on and off, showing her little teeth.

I get out of bed naked and put on the blue-and-green striped robe I found hanging on the back of the bathroom door and that I always leave at the end of the bed. I wave at my daughter, cross under the archway separating the bedroom from the living room, open the door, and lean out halfway. At the very top of the stairs, five steps above me, in front of a worn-out, blue van, a guy in a white tracksuit with a slight belly lights a cigarette and glances at his black digital watch. The supermarket delivery man, I'm guessing. A practical guy who avoids the inner-workings of watches with hour hands, I tell myself; it's a cheap metaphor, but it's shiny.

I gesture for him to come down. He nods and I get that he'll be right in. I go inside and make coffee. There's no need to ask if he wants any to know that he will.

Honey, do you think if I write this it'll seem like a novel? Will it keep the plot moving? If the saltpeter isn't bothering me, don't you think it's because I don't need to write anymore? Should I save these little details for the end? Like how I sleep naked now, which I never enjoyed before. Or saying I want my hair to get tangled. Getting the bottom of my jeans wet with salty water and writing that it doesn't matter one bit. Or how I've changed so much, and so quickly?

No one reads me now.

I'm writing in a *caseta* and I can no longer say, night after night, Honey, take a look at this and tell me if it's moving in the right direction.

I hadn't realized that the other part of you, the one who took up less space, was taking over. Like that idiotic phrase about good things coming in small packages, the "little" part of you was huge, the "big" part of you was small.

Would you say that loving and not being scared are the same thing?

Come look at the sea from over here, help me out, won't you? The sea's lively today and the surfers can't get enough of it, right?

I fell in love with the gigantic little-you because it felt good being there, with him. Not like the comfort of sitting in an armchair but more like carrying around someone who doesn't weigh much. Afterward I'd want to rest for a while but I'd have nowhere to go so I'd get annoyed. With you. And you'd say, I'm sorry.

Mar, hanging in her carrier, nips at the skin between my breasts, leaving wet, red marks, drooling all over me with her fleshy tongue. I smile at the sun and keep walking. The breeze feels intimidated and can't hold my gaze.

I get lost in the southern part of town, past the port, circling around the same stretch of coast that moves through the wild grasses skirting a majestic rock. My fuchsia New Balances aren't right for the setting, but they work for me.

I loosen the strap on the carrier to lower my daughter's little body and take out my breast. She grabs it with both hands and I look at her wrists, marked off by a groove between flesh and flesh. She lowers her head, protected by the floral hat, and sucks. We walk along like that, with the sea at our feet and the sky covering our backs and our pain.

The sound of her mouth throws everything off— how I walk, the breaking of the waves, my heart-beat—but it calms me.

Being a mother, for example, is just that.

When I'd tell you, I don't want to mother you, don't make me act like your mother, I was referring to reminding you about things, organizing the draw-ers of your right hemisphere, ordering you to cut your embarrassing nails, asking you to do your share of the chores, and letting me enjoy my half of our marital rights.

Which meant just being who I was, taking the reins, keeping my crystal ball, envisioning alternate pasts, making you chew everything over and making me hate myself. Hating myself. Hating you.

With your hair long like that, Samson, it seems like you would have understood me by now. But I was too late.

What I mean is that mothering isn't in the dictionary.

I dream I can't breathe and wake up, but I really can't breathe and can't open my eyes. I have some kind of mask, wet and fleshy, on my face. It's clutching me lovingly and I can't breathe. I know it won't do me any harm, I know it's loving me and that it wants to live with me. I know that if I wanted to, I could peel it off my face and breathe right away, but I don't feel like it. I'd rather stay like this, suffocate and pass on, into another life with this thing on my face, making love to me.

I think about my daughter, I reach out my hand and touch her thigh, tell myself I have to move on.

I bring my hands to my face and tear off the thing that's stuck to me. I get a few breaths in and open my eyes. I look at it. It's the starfish. Reddish orange, its body covered in hard, white spots. Each of its five arms is trimmed in a garland of spines. I know the thing at its center is a mouth that looks like it's smiling. Can it survive outside the water? I don't think so.

It's the middle of the night. I take my sleeping baby in one arm, set her on my hip and, naked, with the star in my other hand, leave the house, climb down the stairs, cross through the wide cove right up to the still water, walk five or six steps inward, bend down, and let the star sink to the bottom, under the sand.

Back at the house, I stretch out in bed with my arms around Mar and breathe in and no, it hadn't been a dream. I just abandoned a star that wanted to live with me.

When we arrived—do you remember?—there were a couple people in the *casetes* but the restaurant and hotel were empty, dead, closed like they are now. We were having lunch on the only bench at the south-ernmost end of the beach, behind the two showers, beneath the cascade of balconies and bricks at the blue-and-white restaurant built all the way out to the rocks. I said, I want to check out a nearby hotel and see if I can stay here for a few days, I want to write here. We walked the beach from end to end and as we approached the hotel you said, Fuck, I've got a bad feeling about this, it seems super empty, it's almost scary, right?

At the beginning of my stay here I thought the cove was the shape of a waning moon. Now I think it's only a parenthesis. It opens over here and I don't know where it closes. The endpoints of the paren-thesis are the hotel and restaurant, always closed off, keeping people out. The strip of *casetes* forms the symbol's actual shape, from end to end, no space in-between. That's where I sleep, holding your daughter, mothering, without expecting her to come and hug me.

When I get in the water, naked or in my under-wear, I walk until it comes up to my knees and I get no further because I'm carrying Mar—how lovingly her round, little body grabs at me, her legs, arms, and fingers, my little koala. I can't write or read the message that this parenthesis holds because Mar anchors me to the sand; she still doesn't know how to swim. Mothering forces me to stay here and keeps me from even wanting to know. I must stay here.

I suspect the horizon is the closing parenthesis, that there's silence in between, nothing more—but at the same time that seems all too easy. I want to search for answers at my own pace. I still have pages left to do so.

For the moment I'll stay just like this. Here.

I've slept in spells, the full moon's out and the sea is restless, the sun's not even up yet and I hurry to town, out of breath as I make my way to Aina's patio and sit down on the steps out front.

Mar laughs. She's in bright pink clothes and I'm dressed in yellow.

I get out my laptop, type in my password, and google: "Mediterranean starfish." I look at images, compare them, keep searching.

The star that loves me is, without a doubt, an *Astropecten aranciacus*.

I take Mar out of the white scarf, which I lay on the porch for her to sit on with her stuffed Nemo. She grabs it by the tail and bops it against the ground again and again, laughing all the while. Then she hugs it and sings out the vowels to it in different melodies. She can sit up all on her own, but she still can't crawl.

I read for a while, I aimlessly surf through web pages in one language then another, I watch videos and look at more images, and I learn that this type of starfish can completely self-regenerate from a single arm. I also discover that they're males when they're young and turn into females once they mature. I laugh.

Mar kisses Nemo, whose one fin is smaller than the other.

The Skype icon flashes. My husband's calling from hell. I slam my laptop closed, like he always told me not to.

Mar starts crying and her tears are my punishment. The sun blinds me from below.

The town is so small that we walked around it three or four times on our first day there. The white church—with its squared tower, sharp vertices, and pyramid-like crest—would peek out from some of the street corners and we kept saying that we'd go there. Mostly me, I wanted to go there. I don't know what it is about temples that speaks to me.

I didn't want to make any decisions or set the pace. I didn't want to take the lead. I let myself be dragged under the timid sun. The intersections tested you. Dressed all in white, with your shirt on inside out, you'd say Up there, you'd say Now down there, you'd say Now turn left, and you'd say Now turn right, and off you'd go, carrying your official man card, which not everyone gets when they turn eighteen.

Mar was sleeping and now I can't remember if you had the sling or if I did. Sometimes, when she was sleeping, we wouldn't think about her and it was as if we were alone in the world. We only had to speak softly. Sometimes I'd kiss her head so she knew we wouldn't forget about her, even as she dreamt. The same thing happens now that we're on our own. I have memories where it seems like she wasn't even there, when in reality our bodies have hardly ever separated. Often, when you'd both go off to take a walk and I'd stay home, it seemed like she was still here the whole time but I just wasn't paying attention to her.

When we got to the church, I jumped up the stone stairs two at a time. In six or seven lunges, I reached the door under the portico. Right next to it was a bulletin board with posters tacked up, and I wanted to know everything—everything, because an unspoken novel was developing in my head. I read: *Saint Mary, Star of the Sea*. And I thought: Fuck, how lovely, right? But I didn't tell you.

Today, around mid-morning, I went back there, walking barefoot from the beach up to the highest part of town, near the road, with my sleeping baby in tow. I wanted to ask the saint to care for my star. And to care for my child when I'm not all there.

I knelt down near the entrance because the door was locked. My knee, now red, had set fire to the stone, which shone from the many steps of the faithful.

The sky was that kind of white that won't let the sun through, the kind that blinds you, makes you sweat. I had trouble extending my knees and standing up because Mar already weighs twenty pounds.

Before I left, I remembered that the first time we visited this place, I had spied the thick, firm stem of a rosebush—no leaves, no roses, only thorns—near the leftmost part of the white arch holding up the portico. Today it was lush, spring-like, in bloom. I decided to extend my left arm and drive a thorn into the tip of my middle finger. I'm not even sure I want to know why.

When I wore my wedding ring, I'd put it on my middle finger because it'd fall off my ring finger. It was always falling off. It was too big for me. Way too big.

I married you when my belly was already eight-months along. Mar held still the entire ceremony because she sensed, I'm assuming, that something important was going on outside. I weighed 150 pounds and had a ring size of seven. After giving birth, when I already weighed around 116 pounds, we resized it to a four, but just a short time afterward I weighed 100 pounds and it was too big again. In my purse I carry that extra piece of white gold, wrapped in tissue paper, inside a clear baggy. I never take it out. It makes me nervous.

The ring was always falling off.

It would fall off without me knowing and clank against things. It would leave my ring finger and reappear on the ground. One day I realized that the diamond had fallen out from all the times it had hit the ground—maybe it was under the fridge, which I didn't dare move. I realized there was a hole where the stone had been. And I kept the hole—or the nothingness—in my purse, next to that bit of white gold.

That's why I wound up wearing the ring near my heart, because it fell off me. But it hurt me to see the hole and we were already living apart, and, who knows, in the end I took it off and put it away in a little, round cardboard box covered in cat drawings, and I told you, Look, I put it away in here and when you think it's the right time, when you think we're healed and all that, come and replace the diamond for me.

I can't handle anything else.

I can't write any more.

I'm getting up to open up my purse. I prop up Mar's half-sleeping body with my left arm and she keeps breastfeeding. I'm opening the zipper with my mouth, with my teeth. I'm taking the clear plastic baggy out with one hand and my heart trembles. Coins fall out and Mar opens her eyes wide. I unfold the white paper and look at the piece of metal. I can't breathe. It's much bigger than I remember. The edges of the setting prick.

It's 3:00 A.M. and I can't sleep. It's stifling and the sea won't go to sleep. I can hear their cackling and howling from bed. On the nightstand, there's a photo of my husband leaning against the lamp, with that Playmobil cowboy hat glued onto it. Calling on Skype. Who does that?

Naked, I cross the small living room toward the front wall, where I lean against the windowsill and stare out at the bleak sea. I stick my head and breasts out. On the sand, a starfish edges toward my *caseta*. I once read that they only survive a few minutes outside the water, but this one's stubborn, like Lali—who came over like a mom with a bunch of bags in tow so she could take my dirty laundry, only to see I'd never meant to keep my promise. Or like me—I'd washed my clothes by hand to force her to come. Or like Mar—who wants my boob wants my boob wants my boob.

Near the shore, the two young guys who were smoking hash the other day and the three girls I saw

the first time I came here with my husband—one
with her head shaved like the guys, one with a long
mane, and the third with a braid—pass around a
soda bottle, presumably filled with rum and coke.
They horse around and laugh. The one with the
braid, tall as a beanstalk, stands up and pokes her
bare feet in the water, but she lets out a squeal and
retreats.

I wish I were sixteen again—but *actually* sixteen,
not a measured sixteen.

The Black guy isn't wearing a shirt, just jeans, and
he calls out like he's got eyes in the back of his head:

"Hey, window lady, come down if you want a
sip!"

But then I guess he remembers I'm not alone, so
he turns my way and says: "Hold on! I'll come up!"

My fear of men.

It abandons me when I notice one of the girls
running behind him—the long-haired, pale one in
a miniskirt, knee-high leather boots, and a white,
knit sweater. She catches up to him and slings her
arm around his shoulder.

I take advantage of their walk to go back to my
room, tie on the striped robe, and cover Mar with
a sheet—she's sleeping like a rock.

"Should we go upstairs or are you coming down?"
I hear through the front windows.

I think about whether we'll wake her if they
come in. I think about leaving her alone.

Back in the living room, I peer out the right-side window, smile, and wave for them to come up. They do.

He points at the bed and signals for the girl to keep quiet. They sit at the table, on two of the red chairs, and try not to make a sound. She twirls a lock around her finger and sticks it in her mouth as he takes out the hash and lighter and starts letting it burn. I go into the room, open the window that looks out over the back street—the green railing will keep my daughter safe—and head back to the living room to sit with them.

"Can I have some water?"

I nod and point to the water bottle sitting on the kitchen counter, right over there. The girl stands up and serves herself a glass, drinks it in one gulp, and sits back down. She peers at me. I sense that the silence is weighing down on her chest a little, making her gaze heavy. He pastes two pieces of rolling paper in a V shape with his spit, unhurried, not lifting his eyes. I'm hypnotized by his very black hands handling the white paper against the flower-print oilcloth.

"Do you have a baby?" she asks.

"Yeah, he's on the bed. Look," he whispers.

She's a girl, but who cares.

"What's your name?" The girl crosses her arms in front of her chest—her breasts are significant.

"She doesn't talk." He's referring to me, I think.

"What do you mean, she doesn't talk?"

"I mean she's mute. Can't you tell?"

"Mute?" She uncrosses her arms but keeps her elbows glued to her waist. "But she's not deaf."

"And what's it to you? She's just mute."

I smile at him.

Mute. I hadn't fully realized, though I had my suspicions, but yes, it feels okay and I could keep this going.

He lights the joint and takes three, full drags. His black chest—shiny and bare—fills and then deflates. He passes it to me.

I want to be sixteen.

I take a drag and pass it onto the girl. When she reaches out her hand to take it, she lifts her butt from the chair, leans her body over the table's edge, and plants a kiss on my cheek.

"Your robe is cool," she says, meeting my gaze, a smile in her eyes.

It's fucking hard to find someone who won't mother you or want you to adopt them. We pull each other like magnets.

As they leave, I grab the star—already on the last step to my door—and give it to the girl, who tells me not to worry, that she'll put it back in the ocean.

I want you to know my tongue still hurts, a lot. I haven't been able to eat all that well since the time I bit myself at Bar dels Pescadors. It stings.

It hurt for a few days, as you know, but then it got worse.

Now I write because I can no longer speak.

My arm's asleep. The left one; I slept on it and now I can't move it. I roll in bed, toward the edge, peeling my body from my daughter's, and I try to lift my arm, open and close my hand, but it won't move and my hand's turning purple. The purple starts at my near-black ring finger, flowing from the exact point where the rose bush pricked me at the Church of Saint Mary, Star of the Sea.

David, the supermarket delivery man, honks his horn. I know it's him because I hear him parking without maneuvering back and forth. He turns off the engine and gets out, slams the door shut.

"*Neeeena!* I'm here!" I hear him yell from the window out back. "You gonna make me some coffee, riiiight?"

I sit up, Mar wakes up and smiles. My arm just hangs there while the purple unhurriedly spreads toward my shoulder. Fuck, so now I'm supposed to do everything with just my right arm? I hear him coming down the five stairs to the front door, whistling the whole time.

"Where aaaaare you?" He raps his knuckles on the green door.

I manage to put on my robe using only my right

hand and teeth, barely managing to tie it closed. He keeps knocking, trying out different beats. I grab Mar with my right arm, set her down on my hip, and open the door with my hand, struggling all the while.

The sun's already high and it blinds me. David's got just one bag in each hand.

"About time, *guapa*. Now I get why you put in such tiny orders, so I'll come over more often, right?" He winks at me, speaks in a mix of Andaluz and Catalan. "You're a smart cookie. Just want to remind you that deliveries cost you more that way, eh? But I'm all for it. Just make me one of your special cups of coffee and I'm all for it. Need help with that?"

I'm just standing there, thinking about how I'll manage to put Mar in her highchair, make coffee, and put away the groceries with only one hand. David lowers his eyes, trying to follow my gaze.

"Shit. Your . . . is something wrong?"

A tear gets past me. David doesn't scare me because he's wearing white sweatpants, doesn't shave, has a belly, and sometimes seems like a virgin, though I don't really believe that; maybe he's the secret lover of a supermarket cashier, one who's married with kids, or maybe he's the one married with children. He puts the grocery bags on the table.

"What's wrong, *nena*?" He takes my hand, looks at it from close up, rolls up my sleeve, examines my arm, black by now. "Shit, a doctor should look at this."

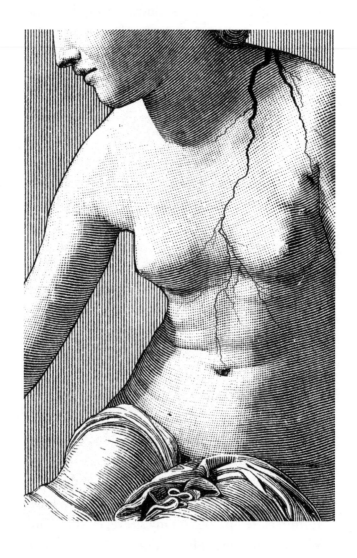

I shake my head. I'm scared. No doctors. I want a natural birth. I asked for one in writing and was ignored.

He puts his hands on my chest, on my robe's neckline flaps.

"May I?"

Mar says yes with a guttural sound and he opens the robe, my breasts exposed. My left breast is purple and a crack runs down from my shoulder, it moves between my breasts and traces the underside of the left. My breast is turning black, the crack grows deeper, and the weight of my arm in David's hands slackens, it breaks off, and it falls to the ground, like ash. The gown falls to my side, secured only by my right shoulder and the belt. My heart hangs there, still joined to my body, unprotected, pumping blood, bum-bum, bum-bum, red-hot.

David's white as a sheet. To be honest, though, I'm just fine. I thought losing an arm or a breast would be a huge deal, but no, it really isn't. That is, beyond the practicalities. Mar examines the dust on the floor, the remains of my arm, and chuckles, crowing in delight. All of a sudden David bursts into idiotic laughter and I can't help myself, I join along, doubling down. He puts his hand on my remaining shoulder:

"I'll make the coffee, *mujer*, don't you worry. What should we do with the baby?"

For the first time in my life, I let myself be cared for. By a man.

Stop calling me.

Let me turn on my cell phone without you calling right away.

You're dead; your voice sears.

It scares me.

I'm a widow with no ring, a mother, alone, a-lone.

I've had stitches in my crotch since your daughter's birth, and it hurts. The scar has healed as it should but it hurts. Let me be. Father me, just for a while, won't you?

I wake up sucking my thumb. There's a wet pressure against my naked crotch. I move my hand away from my mouth and—eyes still closed, expecting the worst—I touch it. With the tips of my fingers, I can feel the starfish's grainy texture clamped against my vagina. I trace her body with my fingertips. I knew it. She's missing an arm. I'm being stalked by a life of connotations.

I try to tear her off me, but her mouth is suctioned to my clitoris and the white thorns that run along her arms are pinning down my groin.

I open my eyes. Mar breathes heavily against the filthy sheets, her belly moving up and down. She turns toward the window and covers her head with her right arm. I get up and look at the star. I feel like she's mistreating me. This isn't love and I don't want it. I tug at her hard, with all five fingers, and try to peel her off. It hurts to pull, but I don't want her on me. Then the star relaxes her grip and I get her off. She's left bruises everywhere. When I inspect her in my hand, so patient and resigned, I feel sorry for her—poor thing.

I'm tired of taking her back to the sea every time she creeps inside my house. If she wants to live with me, fine. I leave her on the nightstand and telepathically ask that she not hurt my daughter. I get up, follow the arched wall in the middle of the room with my gaze, all the way to the windows on the other side, and see that the beach is empty. The rough sea has dusted off its stubborn surfers. I go to the bathroom and grab the white bucket with a pair of green, horizontal lines. Nude and one-armed, I exit the *caseta*, head down the stairs, and cross the sandy beach to fill the bucket with raging seawater.

When I stand back, my heart's left parenthesis flutters. I look out at the horizon and understand that, no, nothing's this easy. I'll have to find my right parenthesis on my own.

When we first started dating, you gestured with your hands so much that you'd knock over wine glasses.

The first time I said, Come over for dinner and we'll go shopping and cook together, you said, Okay,

but no one taught me to cook and I wasn't even allowed to touch the knives. I laughed affectionately. I saw it as an adventure, but really a cyst was born.

Inside the cyst, there's you and me, facing one another. Each of us holds onto our own wheel, like the clock cogs in *Modern Times*, which we push up against the other's. Their teeth mesh seamlessly, rotten teeth against baby teeth. Fatherhood hunches your shoulders forward, maternity pushes up against my back. We turn the wheels, one against the other, and it all rotates in unison, but with all the junk between us, we barely catch a glimpse of one another.

The cyst is also filled with lubricating oil—it fills our nostrils and won't let us breathe.

These days, my school friends often come to mind. Especially those who've changed. When I chop fennel—this I can do myself, single-handedly, hack, hack, hack—Sandra Ribes Palau and Carles Peris Contell, Jordi Soler Rocafull, and Lídia Politi Oltra pop up in my head. Their photos on social media today blend in with the few images I keep as memories, faded and out of focus, like film recorded on a Super 8. Playbacks and sticker books.

I wish I could get to know them again. Once-threatening kids are now queer, esoteric, anarchist, chatty, or well-off adults, or just people trying to find their way. All kinds of people. All kinds among those class clowns I'd hide from while I got straight As and played queen of the playground.

I get tired of writing about lesbian moms and creaky closets. I want to write about my angry and cowardly heterosexuality.

My heart won't dry up outside my body. Not for the breeze nor for the sun, ah, no.

Decked in green polka dots, sitting out on Aina's porch, Mar frowns. She looks at me and ignores Nemo, the flowers, the white cat purring on her leg. I pick her up and help her get on all fours like a cat, thinking maybe she'll crawl, but she doesn't. She's growing so quickly.

It seems like I spent an entire lifetime at school. That it only just ended. But all the cells in our bodies have already regenerated twice since we last saw each other. I keep looking at school pictures on my phone: they've all got the same eyes and now they can see the whole me. So what?

My dead husband keeps insisting with the Skype calls every time I go online. How can I stop it from logging in on its own? Maybe he shouldn't have left without an explanation.

My vagina hurts.

You'd bite.

I'm the one who'd open my mouth wide, but you're the one who'd bite.

When we got back home after spending the day here, we found the female cat was wounded. She'd gotten along with the other cat for years, and they'd always tolerated each other well enough. She'd hiss and he'd swat at her head and then she'd huff and puff, but they'd get on. But lately their relationship seemed more tense, and since he was the youngest, we tried to get another family to adopt him via social media, to no avail.

We got back to the apartment that day to find that he'd bitten her, and she was still bleeding. He'd left two deep punctures in her fur, like a vampire bite. The vet said she'd never seen anything like it. The vet wore a black toga and read the rights and obligations of the institution of marriage out loud to the cat; then I told you, That's enough, you need to go, we need some time apart to think, and take the cat with you.

And then you forgot your Playmobil cowboy on purpose, as your representative, wanted, with no hat.

From that point on, until your dying day, we lived apart.

Lali invited us over for tea.

She'd stopped by to pick up the dirty clothes, but I was out. She popped right in, left a note on the table inviting us over, and even took the dirty diapers with her. I only realized it after I got back from my walk through the rocks along the southern tip of my left parenthesis.

We leave the *caseta* on time, clean and well rested, dressed in yellow, my hair unkempt, and climb up the steps. We tread the asphalt under the white sun and head up to town. Lali lives in the attic of a beige building, ugly and new, hanging from a crag that shoots up from the port. A toylike lighthouse stands next to it.

Lucky there's an elevator—my groin has started hurting quite a bit ever since the star attached herself to me.

I'm embarrassed to show up without an arm.

"Come on in, ladies."

She's wearing the same thing as usual: the same old apron over her same old printed dress. She's put pink, plastic rollers in her orangey-red hair in an attempt to tame her frizz.

"What happened?" she asks, pointing to my empty, yellow sleeve, like someone asking about a cold after a sneeze.

I hunch my shoulders.

"Dear Lord, this young lady needs to learn to take care of herself."

I follow her to the glassed-in balcony, the reflection of the water in the port bouncing off the panes. She has an American-style bar.

"Sit." She points to one of the two green chairs. It's velvet, just like the one my grandmother had in her dining room when I was little.

There's a sturdy, green chair in all of my novels, I just can't help myself. I picture myself at age five,

brushing the velvet back with my palms and then
tracing my initials in the opposite direction, with one
finger.

I sit down and lift Mar out of the white scarf tied
around my body. Lali takes her and puts her on her
lap. Mar claps and laughs.

"She's not crawling yet?"

I shake my head.

"I've seen the starfish thing before. I mean, the
thing with your arm. I've never seen a maimed mute
before. But that's okay."

You sure know a lot about starfish, but the
red-orange in your hair is fake and your roots are
showing, I tell her in my head, to myself.

She stands up.

"Coffee or tea?"

I smile.

"Tea, then," she decides. "Green? Green. You can
pick up the clothes later. I've got them all set: they're
dried and folded in the bag. Don't worry—you can
carry it all with one hand," she winks.

I hope she won't add lemon; the wound on my
tongue still burns.

She has green eyes. I hadn't noticed. A mature
green, a freshness from another time. She smells like
forest.

"I went over to do some berry picking today.
There's already some growing on the road a bit farther up. Want some?"

Without waiting for an answer, she brings over a

plate and sets it on the little marble table, between the two chairs.

The road. The train. Red stains that won't wash out. I haven't had my period again since I gave birth. I'd forgotten how to leave here: on a train. I can't remember how many days it's been since I arrived.

Lali has two arms and hustles and bustles with Mar on her hip. They're good together.

"Have you seen Aineta?"

I shake my head. All I need from Aina is her WiFi. She's a WiFi character. Lali the mother, the pot-smoking kids, the harmless delivery guy. That's it. Enough for a constellation.

Lali won't sit down even for a moment.

"Want me to fix your hair?" she asks, but doesn't wait for an answer.

I can feel the blunt teeth tugging down from crown to nape.

"Look, Mar, fix Mommy's hair. Grab the comb, honey."

I draw back, quick. No. Not the baby. I fix my baby's hair. The baby won't fix mine. Let's not play that game. To each her own. Lali quickly gets the point.

With her round but stubborn fingers, Mar tangles up my hair while Lali attempts to fix it. That's better.

I eat a berry, sip some tea, and let my eyes fall over the quiet and sunny port.

Wherever we'd go, we'd look out for the "for-sale" signs. We also liked "for-rent" signs, just not as much.

One question you learned in some class—I can't remember which—was: What are you *not* thinking about when you think about X? You'd stress the "not." You'd ask yourself that question often. In your case, it was always a part of your past.

What were we not thinking about when we were looking to buy a place?

My fingers are frozen on the keyboard. Imagine just one hand, because that's all I have to write with now and, yes, it's slow going.

Did you know some people call up real-estate agencies and check out apartments for sale with no intent of buying, just for fun? As a hobby, I find it thrilling. Better than golf, movies, making love. It's free, tactile fiction—and it isn't scary.

I know. While we amused ourselves with looking for a house to buy, we wouldn't think about the dizzying notion that you were my home, or that I was yours, or that the two of us, together, were Mar's.

At Casetes Beach we only found one sign, and it wasn't on the beach.

The fact that I can't live here, and wouldn't ever want to, is probably why this is the perfect place to write this short parenthetical—frayed and patched back up single handedly—this open parenthesis whose ending I don't know.

I suppose my legs will fall off soon. My groin and hip have gone dead to the touch since I woke up mounted by the star, so before I'm left with no lower extremities, I want to walk to town. I have things to do. After that, I doubt I'll be able to walk again and it'll take a miracle for me to leave this beach.

Will I die here?

I know I won't. But I write down questions so I'll seem more interesting.

I change the bucket water for the starfish who wakes up next to me every day, in my bed, gasping for air as she rests an arm on my only shoulder. I place her in the bucket and caress her now-asymmetric center. Two of her four legs have changed from reddish orange to gray.

I wrap myself in the pink, somewhat elastic scarf that Lali keeps in the closet to make an ergonomic seat for the baby, who's dressed in a simple pistachio onesie today. I tie a sturdy knot, grab my laptop, and exit the *caseta*, taking the path upward as I leave behind a gray sea of choppy foam. The dense, silky clouds blot out the sun, but the glare still blinds me.

Mar sings to herself and falls asleep.

I stop by Aina's porch and put in an order at the supermarket so that David will come. I need to talk to him. We'll see how that goes, what with the wound on my tongue that hasn't healed and this idiotic but perhaps false certainty that I won't ever be able to improve upon silence.

Later, as the sky turns overcast, I ring Lali's intercom and drop a hand-written note in her mailbox: "I won't be able to stop by anymore. Come see me, dearest dear." I know she will. It's nice not having to doubt it.

Finally, I head to the church, not to pray for my incomplete body—I don't want it to stop, now that it's begun—but because there's a chest of drawers I want in one of the dumpsters in front of the church. I know it must be there, waiting for me. Dragging it all the way back to the *caseta* will be my legs' final quest.

The sky's first drops start falling, thick and hot.

It happened when we walked outside the church. It all started with, People are such pigs. On the sidewalk out front was your typical dumpster overflowing with dusty old furniture. We'd always complain when we'd see a dumpster but then we'd always run right up to it because we knew that, cast about among all the crap, we'd find strange yet conceivable pasts, and our own possible futures. We'd end up leaving everything there, of course, but the fiction of it all drew us in so deeply that we couldn't help it. Inventing separate lives was one of the few delicious bugs we'd caught in the spider web between us, the only tooth in the cog—no, one of the two, the other was sex—that didn't need to be polished, smashed, shaped, or unchained.

And there it was. A simple, wooden chest of drawers, old and dusty, tall and narrow, veneered and varnished, inlaid with marquetry. You asked, Have the termites gotten to it? And I made sure they hadn't. I pulled on the top handle, the highest up of its eight or nine golden knobs, which gave it a rococo air. It looked like the first drawer was dragging the second one open with it, but what was really happening was that the two were actually connected, and they moved as one piece. They advanced like that, a united front budging toward me, and then I managed to separate the magnets holding them together with a shove, until the top lay flat, like a table, like a vanity. Inside—in a seven-by-four grid—twenty-eight compartments awaited me, all with corresponding golden handles, all empty. I want it, I thought.

Do you want it?, you asked, in blinding white. We'll take it with us, you said. I looked at you like you were crazy, but you insisted. Seriously, I'll grab it and drag it to the train, okay? It must have weighed fifty or sixty pounds or something like that. I thought it was a dumb idea. Now I wish I had a keepsake of that stupid thing you'd done, done for me. To stash my words away there.

I arrive at the church, my crotch necrotic and my legs all pins and needles, and look into the dumpster out front. The chest is still there. If I don't get my act together, the rain will ruin it.

I put my laptop in one of the drawers. I open the false top drawer, which drags out the one below it, and the chest transforms into a pull-out secretary, offering up its twenty-eight compartments. I wonder what might be in—what I should put in—the two extra compartments. I undo the knot on the pink scarf, pulling Mar out of it as she wakes up and laughs, and place her on my back before tying it again. It's amazing what I've learned to do with just one hand. I get by with my chin and teeth. I start hauling the chest of drawers, which weighs as much as a half-written novel, toward the beach.

When I reach the first street corner, already panting and partly soaked from the rain, I run into the pale girl from the other night, the one with long hair. She's wearing black leggings, a huge, pink T-shirt, fuchsia sneakers like my own, and a high ponytail. She looks at the heart that hangs outside of my body, and the arm that isn't there.

"Can I help?"

Why even ask? Why not just do it already? I don't want to nod. I want to tell her to do whatever the fuck she wants, that if what she's after is my approval, my "you're a good kid," then she should keep smoking hash. I want to tell her that I used to smoke hash to feel rebellious but all I ever got was approval and that's why I still want to be sixteen and not give a shit about anything. I can't improve upon the silence and my tongue hurts. She doesn't wait for an answer to start helping. Of course I want her help.

Thunder calls down its threat from the sky, it wants to rain down on us even harder, I see the girl's hands rising up to the clouds behind my shoulders.

We reach the street behind the row of *casetes* and right in front of us five steps lead down to my front door. We can't get it through the upper window because of the lattice-work. She's already noticed that my legs are giving out—plus I only have one arm and I'm carrying the baby, who has fallen asleep—so she grabs the lower part so that she can carry more of the weight. I let her because she's not my daughter and sometimes you shouldn't let metaphors go that far.

When the girl leaves, climbing two stairs at a time in her fuchsia sneakers, I lay Mar on the bed. The drumming of the raindrops on the roof, thick and quickening, dusts the sleep from her eyes. She perks up. I wipe the chest of drawers, dry it off a bit, pull out the top drawer and open up the compartments, row by row, one by one. There they all are, waiting for me.

a b c d e f g

h i j k l m n

o p q r s t u

v w x y z

And I still have two compartments left to open.

At 27, like I suspected, a left parenthesis, (.

I don't need to open the last one to know it's empty.

One evening, in the days between our trip to Casetes Beach and your death, you came home for dinner. The baby was asleep and the two of us stood out on the terrace drinking white wine that was too cold, with our elbows leaning on the railing as we looked out at the sea, a mile away, flooded with moonlight. I was wearing my lilac-patterned nursing pajamas and you were in tracksuit bottoms and a red T-shirt.

You said, I understand my novel now, the one I'm writing, the internal conflict and all, I've been turning it over in my mind. And me: What, come on, let's hear it. Then you told me, Well, the beggar, who has to bury his friend, and the friend, aren't the man-me and boy-me, it's not me burying the child part of myself, like I thought. No?, I asked without looking up at you, before taking a sip. Really, it's that I'm burying the inner part of myself that wants to be my own father, or grandfather, that tells me how I should do this or that, that wants to control and command me. It's like I have to bury that part of me to stop being a child, do you see what I mean?

You were unbelievable.

You were just too much.

You were still a boy and you were already too much.

Back then I thought, Look how smart he is, my husband. And for a while you talked about your father and grandfather and your childhood and adolescence. And how there was a part of both of them in that warped and incomplete part of you—the part you wanted to bury.

The next morning—in the early hours, wide-awake, while Mar was breastfeeding and the moon was fading, in a bed emptied of you—I realized that your mother was also in that part of you being buried and, naturally, a huge part of me was there, too.

The mother-of-my-husband-me in a splintered coffin, organs missing, about to be buried alongside you. You ran right past me.

Getting dizzy. Falling short. Off and running.

I came here to write, to close a parenthesis with a sign I can't find, to die, to bury myself, to come back to life, and not at your command. I'll be the one to bury myself. That much I know.

At first light, close to the crystal-clear sea, I spread my blue sarong out on the sand and set Mar down, in her yellow bathing suit, alongside her orphaned and crippled Nemo. I give her a kiss and put on her little flowered hat and sunblock in case we lose track of time.

In my bikini—but only the bottoms, because the top seems stupid when you only have one boob—I start digging with my only hand. I feel embarrassed because there are a couple of girls in white bottoms flirting about ten feet away, but I steel my heart,

which is now hanging out of my rigid and desic-
cating sternum.

After a while, the sun's already bearing down on
me, I'm sweating, my fingernails hurt. Out of bore-
dom, Mar complains until she pulls the left parenthesis—the one I thought was in the drawer—out of
her mouth, and then starts combing the sand with
it, looking for its counterpart.

I'm on my hands and knees when, there in front
of me, the shadows of two heads and two backs
appear. I look up. The two girls in bottoms, one
with bangs and the other with curls, close in on me
with a smile. I lower my eyes and keep digging.

They don't ask but they expect me to invite them
over. At this point, asking for Lali, demanding her
presence, wouldn't improve upon the silence either,
so I'll have to welcome them to the farewell party
for my legs. They're too young, much like both of
my mothers were when they first met, when I was
already two years old, but maybe that's when they
actually seemed their oldest to me.

I want to learn how to ask for help, I tell myself.
I'm a widow for that very reason, I tell myself. They
won't kneel down if I don't ask them to first, I tell
myself. I look up again, smile, raise an eyebrow,
purse my lips. I hope they get the hint because my
tongue hurts too much.

They nod, mute like me, and kneel down.

We dig, dig, dig, the one with bangs plays with

Mar for a while, singing the vowels to her. We keep digging and then it's there: a hole large enough for a coffin.

I get in it, lay down with my arm wrapped around my body, close my eyes. I feel the sand fall on me, like dry rain. I hear Mar laugh. I feel the weight of more and more sand and stop breathing. I feel the three of them, right there above me, trampling the sand to make sure I'm properly buried.

Take care of Mar for me, it'll only be a little while, I tell them in my head, hoping they'll hear.

I wasn't able to do it on my own after all. But he wasn't the one to bury me, I was right about that much. I'm no longer a girl. I'm no longer a girl forced to act like a mother.

How infuriating, when it seemed like everything was working and the gears were turning again.

People talk a lot about spirals. How it seems like you're passing by the same point when you really aren't, how it might look like it but you aren't really the same, how you're going through it differently, how yes, you're moving forward.

It was infuriating, when everything had been peaceful for a while, and you'd come home now and again, and we'd laugh at our faults and get self-congratulatory because it seemed like you were changing, like I was moving forward, like being parents was easy, like the gears were slowing down, like I could admire you. And then all of a sudden I'd say, I think, and ca-chink, everything would start up again like a well-oiled machine with a timer.

Fuck-ing in-fur-i-at-ing.

The kind of fury that makes you lift one knee and stomp your foot against the ground. I already knew that my legs would be gone when I pulled myself out of the sand. I knew it because my starfish's two arms had looked like they were about to fall off for a while now and because my legs could barely hold me up.

When I thought I'd had enough of being buried, I began to move my hand and my head. Little by little, I dug my way through the sand and made a decent hole. I sat up, bending at the waist, and noticed how it was splitting like a dry tree trunk. The lid of my sand coffin crumbled as I unearthed my head. Mar was sleeping right next to me, on the sarong, snuggled up to her stuffed Nemo. My young mothers were no longer around and their two shadows were slowly fading: the first scissor-shaped, and the second smelling like an eraser. I thanked them for having enough faith to let me come back to life on my own.

No. You wouldn't call this a *rebirth*, not by any means. It's still not that. I'm simply here to leave behind the legs that once lifted me up, to learn to live without pillars a bit, without my excessive firmness. It'll do me some good to drag myself around for a few days. Having to ask for help.

I leave my legs buried there, a gift for my husband, a sign of resignation. Using my hand for support, I pull my breast, my heart, my head, and little else out of the sand. I stretch out by the sea, under a crushing sun, and use my fingertips to dust the sand off my nipple so Mar can breastfeed if she wakes up, and I wait for Lali or David to heed my call.

Muriel, you said, I've been thinking. I've always been bored with your monologues; they're so repetitive and loud. As soon as you announce the subject matter, I know whether to check out right then and there, or not yet.

My challenge, you said, as we climbed up the beach barefoot, heading to the terrace bar at the closed hotel, is to be a man and support myself and my own life. You tapped Mar's shiny little head right as she was starting to fall asleep, tucked in the sling. To stand on my own two feet and not drag other people down—to be happy, dammit, with you and as a father. And *I* didn't zone out, of course not, and I said, I'm moved and I love you so much, honey, without looking you in the eye as I held your hand. Then you stopped me: *Guapa*, you're the most beautiful woman in the world, thank you for walking down this path with me, for staying close to me and letting me get close to you, step by step—you're brave, and I love you so much, too. I dreamt, you concluded, that you were asking me questions. *You* were asking *me* questions! And you laughed.

I managed not to talk, not to let that intensity fade, that intensity that, though recurring, was more intense than ever at that point—less needy, less helpless, more adult and more menacing. You said, I truly believe that I'm just a short way from becoming a man. I know I have to fix a couple bad habits, but I'm on my way. I'm leaving behind that child who's throwing a fit because his mom won't pay attention, leaving behind the teenager who asks, What am I doing?, what am I doing?, and now?, what else should I do? I try to make decisions and sometimes I get it right and sometimes I fuck up, Muri. That's where I'm coming from . . . And do you know where I'm going? I shook my head because I knew there wasn't much life left in you, that you were dying on me, and I barely had a voice left, though I hadn't yet bit my tongue. I'm going where my father is, where yours is, where Captain Reeb and Ned Stark and Don Draper are.

We laughed and Mar stirred for a few seconds, looked around, fluttered her long, black lashes, and sighed before suddenly falling back asleep, letting her head drop on my breast again. You pressed my hand tighter and we picked up the pace. We left the terrace for the asphalt behind it. A salty gust of wind blew all around. We kept going until we reached the hotel's backend, where the two young guys and three girls I still hadn't met were drinking, smoking, dancing to their cell-phone music.

Decked in white, you kept saying, I'm a man, I'm a man, in a low voice, like a mantra, so then I thought I must be a woman and not a mother caring for her boy. You said, I'm not into these people, let's go. But dressed like a rainbow, *I* would have stayed, smoked the hash, drunk the booze, gotten sunburned and done whatever, anything really, just so I wouldn't have to spend my time with a real man.

You were dying on me. Dying in my arms. I hugged Mar.

I'm still here with my sarong laid out on the beach, under the crushing sun, next to a pile of wet sand and a hole, my clapping daughter, a dirty stuffed animal, and a fragmentary starfish who appears to have dragged herself all the way here from the *caseta*. Luckily Mar can't crawl yet and hasn't left my side. It seems she's not the only one needing nine months of exterogestation.

I'm a head, an arm, one breast, one lung, and one heart. Enough to breastfeed and wrap up a novel.

With just one elbow for support, I shield my eyes from the sun with my hand and peer beyond the horizon, looking for something—I don't know

what—maybe an island or a bridge between two
continents, anything that might work as a right
parenthesis. The shimmering sea blinds me though,
and I can't see myself out there.

The first thing I'll ask for when someone comes
around is to have my hair tied up in a ponytail.
From now on, I'll have to ask for a lot of things.
I'm rethinking whether I might have to talk again
or what, before this all ends.

What's falling off next? My head, or my other
arm? What'll be my last piece as this Muriel and
the first of the next one? Asking the star would be
silly because, to the star, all arms are the same, right?

I can hear someone treading the sand but can't
figure out how to turn to look. Mar does and smiles.
Judging by her face, it must be David.

"*Nenaaa*, what are you doing here? Gosh, you're
not doing great, are you?"

"I'm better than ever." I'm shocked by my own
voice. I wasn't expecting it.

"You're talking now?"

"Yes. Stand in front of me, I can't turn around."

David plants himself before me and blocks the
sun. Against the glare, his white tracksuit looks
dark. He scratches his beard.

"Better than ever? Really?"

I laugh, and say, "It's never as dark as just before
the dawn. Did you know that? Someone told me
that once."

"I think that was Batman."

"There you go."

"*Entonces, ¿qué?*. Want some coffee?"

"Let me order it."

"How come?"

"I'm learning to ask. It's my new thing."

"Cool." He folds his arms across his belly.

"David."

"Yes, ma'am."

"Could you please put my hair in a ponytail, get Mar, get me, pick up the sarong, take us home, and run me a bath?"

"Of course, *cariño*. But I'm making myself a coffee, okay?" He bends down, strings a shoelace out of his sneaker and starts fixing my hair.

"Ah. You saved me from quite the sunburn. And Mar, too. Thank you."

"No biggie."

"It *is* a big deal. Thank you."

He kisses me on the mouth, with no suggestiveness at all.

I'll ask David to stay a few days—hopefully he can. Don't think I'm cheating. I need to need, and this'll be good practice. Don't come asking more of me— you died and have no right to get nitpicky now. I have to fend for myself now and that's what I'm trying to do.

I'd forgotten about your ashes.

I can't change Mar's diapers or bathe her. I can't change the water in the starfish's bucket, can't open my laptop, can't go up and down the stairs, can't, can't, can't, and David helps a lot.

I don't need to eat or go to the bathroom because I no longer have that kind of machinery in me.

What I need is to breastfeed and write.

David asked the grocery store for a week off. He says he's learned a lot by my side, that it's all made quite an impression on him, and that I'll return the favor eventually.

"Relax, I'm happy to," he insists whenever I over-thank him. I discovered that, under the *caseta*, in the space behind the columns, between the sand and the foundation, it's really kind of nice—it's a shady, quiet spot.

I also discovered that I can scoot around on one hand, hopping a little, and that depending on some-one who's actually available can feel very healthy. I won't need nine months or eighteen years. I think I'll be fine with just a few days.

After a lot of pleading on social media, and with the help of a friend, we found a couple to adopt our cat. He'd live in a huge country house with other cats and delightful people. It was a little far and you drove there alone, all the way from the apartment where you'd moved when we separated.

The vampire-like bite on the other cat's back had scarred over, and I thought that maybe, once the cat was settled with another family, you could come back and live with us. After all, if you didn't bite me, we could make love again.

It was almost midday when you called from out there, four counties north, to say, I'm coming, we're done here and the cat'll have a blast. You gave me one of your, I'll tell you more laters—and whenever you said that I knew you wouldn't hang up until you'd told me at least three-quarters of the story. You went on and on about how wonderful the couple and the country house were, how you'd hit it right off, how you wished we could both go there together one day, and about the death of another cat.

You'd gotten there late but they said it was better that way, because you'd arrived right when they needed you. A few seconds before you pulled up with our tomcat, their old alpha had let out his dying breath. They wanted to go straight to the vet in case he could be saved, and you'd drive. The cat had died and you said, It's not just that I saw a dead cat, Muriel, it's that I saw it die. You told me you'd had a major epiphany, that one cat would substitute the other, that this was a year of changes, and that you'd tell me all about it when you got back. Then you hung up.

We'd agreed to meet on the boardwalk in an hour and a half, but I knew you wouldn't make it.

I waited with Mar until midafternoon, on a bench on a playground facing the shore, but you never showed up.

Your ashes arrived a few days later.

Seated on the *caseta*'s living-room floor, Mar plays with shells and letters from the drawer that David let her scatter around. I begged her especially not to eat the dot on the "i" and not to lose my left parenthesis. She laughed. My little bubbly one. Dressed in pink and purple, sweaty, barefoot, and tousled. My queen.

David sat me on the highchair because it's at the perfect height for typing with one hand. I spend hours poring over the text and jotting down the last few experiences I've collected. It's like I'm keeping up to date.

I write and unwrite. David lays Mar out on the table every once in a while, so she can breastfeed, and the starfish scuttles around the oilcloth with just two arms, kissing my fingers. Every few minutes, she takes a dip in a silver, oval-shaped plate of sea water.

Today, I got a call from my husband on Skype—a long and insisting one with intermittent messages typed in. "For the love of God, pick up the phone," "Don't you think this has gone on long enough?" All this, despite the fact that my laptop has never gotten WiFi in the *caseta*.

Silence. Everything happens in silence. Big words like *happiness, intensity, companionship, motherhood, fatherhood, love,* and *sex* go by in silence. I-need-si-lence.

I can't stomach casting your ashes out into the sea, calling you, picking up the phone, writing you, logging onto Skype. You're dead and you need to keep quiet. Dead. There won't be mediums—no prayers, no dreams. I don't want to hear you anymore.

I also promise not to talk to you until I've learned this not-a-mother not-a-child language. I promise as I leave my handprint on the sand, spit smack in the middle of it, and then erase it all before dragging myself over to the shade under the *caseta* where David rocks my sleeping baby.

He's not taking your place. Rest assured. He's a husband in training.

Mar and I have decided to spend the night on the faded red sofa out on the terrace. My breast and arm, open like a parenthesis, nurture her with milk and motherhood. She's longer than I am and I can't hold her. My head seeks out the silence among the dried branches and sap cobwebs.

I can hear the high tide in the middle of the night and then my front door closing, followed by David's footsteps making the wood steps creak on the spiral staircase as he climbs up from the bedroom. When he reaches the terrace, he quietly removes his white sneakers, dusts off his feet and lays down beside Mar and me, belly up, fingers laced behind his neck. He contemplates the Milky Way, and I contemplate him. Surely he's thought about asking if I need anything, but knows the only thing I need is to learn how to ask. All three of us breathe.

"I just came up from the far end of the beach, behind the hotel."

"Did you smoke? It's good, right?" I reply.

"Mm. They said it's cool out and that they're heading to a restaurant on the other end, and that you can climb in through a broken window and it's perfect inside."

"You want to go."

"So do you."

We laugh. He looks at me, looks at the baby, looks back at me.

"Come on, ask me, huh?" he prods.

It's hard. I feel like a bad mother and like I'm taking advantage of him, but especially like a bad mother and like an awful, terrible person:

"Could you carry Mar, please?"

He stands up:

"And who's gonna carry you, honey?"

I burst out laughing:

"You?"

He winks.

South of town, past the port, a narrow path snakes through the grass, between a cliff and an imposing, craggy mountain. I'd often go for a walk there, with Mar in tow, when I still had legs. Remember how we'd wandered around there for a while, the day we got here? The path winds and winds and winds, right into a small cove, and we'd ended up there without even realizing it.

You kept on with all that, I'm a man, I'm a man business. After the silence, what I liked most was keeping quiet while I listened to you, when you tried to talk like a grown-up. You said, This place has me feeling inspired, and you took a deep breath. We stopped for a moment to take in the omniscient sea. You said, I've pictured myself a lot, right here, on this stretch of beach, but I didn't know it was here. Now I know, Muriel. Right in front of the water I see the horizon, I see eternity. I'm not afraid of life or death. I'm ready to take my own path, serenely, the only path I can take from now until my death. In that vision, my hair is long and I'm all in white, with shorts and a poorly buttoned shirt. Tattoo showing. And my piercings, too. You take my hand and Mar's already walking, right there in front of us, hopping around and looking for white seashells. I feel the energy radiating from your hand, your warmth. I hold you, let your fingers wander my palm. You smile and the wind blows hair in your face. I never get angry anymore. My back is straight as an arrow and I'm happy. I'm a man.

I never answered anything. I was afraid to let go, to love you as the man you were, and to be happy by your side. Afraid that afterward your child-anger would return and destroy everything again. And I didn't know if I could tame the controlling mother I carried inside of me, who was always saying her piece, who'd declare what she expected, who embroidered the rules, who wanted to give orders, to direct you. I'd think, I should keep quiet, keep even more quiet, but at the same time the silence seemed a sad resignation, a disconnect from reality, from life, from that cove, that cliff. As if silence were an extinguished light bulb, or a flashing light that warns: running on empty.

Don't worry, you said. That you're listening to me is already a big deal and I'm not expecting a reply. Let's take it easy, you said.

Mar woke up and smiled. Her face was sleepy, soft and reddish. I asked you to hold her for a while.

On our way back, we were singing one of your most basic, self-referential compositions: luuuuul-laa-by, for my Maaar, luuuuul-laa-by, for my Maaar . . . and the wind kept us from hearing the footsteps of a passerby with messy hair and a bald spot, laughing under his breath.

"It happened at the market, when I was young. We were still living in Barcelona and my parents ran a

Japanese restaurant, although they were Chinese, you know, the usual. I went with my father to buy some fresh fish. I loved going there, you know?, because the fishmonger always called me handsome. The fish was super fresh, out on the ice counter, at that time of day. That morning . . . it seemed like one of the trout was breathing, I'm telling you, guys, I could see its gills opening and closing, opening and closing. I'm sure that wasn't really the case, since it couldn't have survived so long outside of the water, but I swear I saw it try and open its mouth. I touched it and it was soft, like, really soft, and slimy, it closed its mouth and stopped moving. I tried to find its heartbeat but couldn't. I haven't eaten any meat since then, guys, and I believe in reincarnation. I can't think of any other way to keep on living." He had been serious up till that moment and then he laughed: "That and smoking hash, of course. Pass the joint, dumbass."

His Black friend passed it to him, letting the smoke stream out of his mouth, and said: "Okay, I'll go. It happened yesterday. But it could happen tomorrow, too, yeah? Or in just a few minutes. It's pitch black out, I'm heading home with a stomachful of rum and coke and I'm a little drunk or whatever. You guys always go home down the back streets and I walk across the beach, you know, because I like going home by myself. Okay, so I always do this. It has to be right in the middle of the beach. Not

before or after. I stop in front of *caseta* 17, which I
figure is right smack in the middle, and stand there.
I'm looking out at the water, okay?, right out. Then
I take off my shoes. It doesn't really matter if it's in
the spring like it is now, or in the dead of winter
like a few months ago, yeah? I take off my shoes and
walk right up to the water and put my feet in and
the cold shoots right up my spine. It's like a freak-
ing wave of cold that goes up and up and up, it gets
me hard, it calms my buzz, and leaves me all brrrr-
rrrf, *joder*, *vale*, you know what I mean? Just brutal.
Way more than smoking, guys, I'm serious, you've
gotta try it." He goes quiet and looks at his friends.
"What's wrong? You think it's stupid, or what? Why
are you looking at me like that?" The girl I know
best laughs and applauds. "Oh, okay, fuck, thanks."

I've learned a lot seeing how the most intense
experience of someone's life can be super simple,
recurring, and sought-after.

When we got inside—contorting ourselves
through the window's broken glass—we saw a dimly
lit restaurant with last season's table settings, and
five teenagers circling a round table. The girl with
the braid got up and kindly got us some beer and
orange soda from the shiny refrigerators next to the
door. We—or I should say David, for the both of
us—flung two windows wide open so we wouldn't
drown in smoke and sat down to eat peanuts with
them. Mar was sleeping in David's arms, he set me

down on the table, and he sat down in one of the metal chairs. We didn't want to smoke. I'd proposed doing a round of "the most intense experience of your life" and everyone was immediately joking about how mine was only having an arm and a head.

"No," I laughed. "My most intense experience was giving birth to Mar." We all got serious and I passed the joint without taking a puff. "Being afraid, not being afraid, thinking, 'I can't do it,' thinking, 'Of course I can, I have to be able to, I want to be able to,' making my husband write *I CAN* on one hand and *DO IT* on the other with a marker, allowing the waves of pain to pass over me, coming and going, and wanting them to carry me off with them, getting pissed at the whole team of doctors and nurses, grabbing hold of my man, crying out, letting them cut me, mutilate me, wound me, sew me back up, allowing them to force me to give birth at a specific time out of fear of losing Mar, and finally, above all else, holding her for the first time and saying, 'My little one, my little one . . .' And then forgetting it all. And hours later my man telling me that I'd said, 'My little one, my little one . . .' Her warm little body, bloody and so warm, sticking to my own." I went quiet. I no longer have a belly and I hardly have a chest, just one breast and a heart.

"You said, 'My man.'" David was looking at me, eyes black.

"What?"

"You just said, 'My man.' You never use that word. You always say, 'My husband.'"

His eyes were on fire.

The day I gave birth Roger had been a man. Roger could be a man when he needed to be and I didn't know how to get it through my head. A man. Now I'm dead and buried.

I apologize. It's not always, You're a child, you make me mother you and I'm tired of it. It's not always, I'm a man with a beard who makes decisions and I'll learn how to do it on my own.

Gears. Rust, oil, screeching, lubricant in the water.

Wherever you are, know that I now know that there inside you, under my husband, covered in children's gift wrap, was a man. That I know it's too late. That if I'd seen him, I would have waved, looked him in the eyes, said, Hello, I see you, you exist, you'll do just fine.

Do you think that underneath the girl playing the mother, wrapped in kraft paper, there's a woman who can keep quiet? I think so, yes. Come find me, I'm cold.

Everyone was staring at David, as if there were some unspoken rule about taking turns in a circle around the table. David didn't miss a beat.

"Music is my thing, and jamming out with my

brother. I was a rockstar before I started working at the supermarket, if you can believe it."

"I recognized you a while ago, but I didn't want to come off as some crazy fan. You guys were great, dude," said the girl with the eyebrow piercing, her boots on the white tablecloth, flattering him. "It might have seemed tacky, being a fan of yours, but what can I say? I saw the value in your work. I respected it."

"Thanks. Exactly. I'd write the lyrics and he'd come up with the chords on the guitar. It took a lot of skill. We actually broke up the band because I ran out of things to say. He always followed my lead, for better or worse. When Muriel first suggested playing this game I was thinking mine was singing my favorite song at Palau Sant Jordi—*Tú me rompes las entrañas, me trepas como una araña* . . . —but no. What moved me most was telling the audience that my brother was going to sing that song on his own, with his guitar. It was the only one he'd sing by himself. And the crowd would go nuts. *Loco loco.*" He hugged Mar, who was asleep in her carrier. "And that's that."

I feel bad writing this way because it ends the fragment on a melodramatic note, but if I'm being true to the fiction of it, I should say that David wiped away a tear with the sleeve of his tracksuit.

You had a brother, too. Always remember that. Now that you're no longer around, your brother must remember the Sunday mornings when, as a boy, he'd sneak under your flannel covers and hug you tight. Remember that, too.

You were the typical poet, the one who always played the same handful of tunes on the guitar, and he was the one who'd read easy books but played wonders. The only thing you couldn't see was your own poetry. Dark, gathered, groveling, and gutted, but still poetry, after all. The poetry I fell in love with when you were eighteen. An empty pen equals death.

He'd help us when we'd move. He was the best man at our wedding. Re-mem-ber.

I wish you could have met David.

I wish I'd gone to bed earlier. Depression's always made me sleepy. When I write "depression" I don't mean that terrible affliction psychiatrists diagnose, but just feeling a little sad some days. When I feel that way, I'd rather sleep. Wake up late. Go to bed early. Take long naps.

I wish I'd fallen asleep before noticing the long-haired girl's talking—the one who came to my *caseta* the other day to help me with the chest of drawers.

The other two girls—the one with the buzzcut and the one with a braid—had already shared their own intense experiences: singing a cappella and "fucking," respectively.

Then the one with the glorious mane pierced me with her gaze:

"For me, it was getting to know you." She circled the entire audience with her eyes: "You've all heard that babies smell like babies, right? Well, I say this *senyora* here smells like a mom. Even now, without a body, she smells like a mom. Can't you tell?"

The other five, even David, looked at her with blistering compassion. I glared: she called me *senyora*. And she wasn't done:

"My mom stopped being my mom the day I smelled her shit. I realized her shit stank, like mine."

"Up until a few days ago, I could poop, too, sweetie," I quipped.

"You're not getting it. What I'm saying is that when someone takes care of you, they put up with you, right? I mean, when someone's there for you, they could shit on your hand and you still wouldn't think it stinks."

"Man, why do you have to be so gross?" the Black guy shot back, burning hash.

"Go fuck yourselves," she retorted. "Muriel's acting like she's one of us, but really she's a mom pretending to be one of us. And I don't know. It kind of bugs me that she wants to act all young, but at the same time, I also kind of wish I could adopt her as a mom."

"You mean you want her to adopt you," The girl with the braid raised one eyebrow, gnawing her fingernails.

Then the long-haired girl morphed into a backyard soap-opera star, covered her eyes with her hands, dropped her head, and started bawling:

"My mom drinks alone. It makes me want to ask her to come out with us one night, you know?"

Then it all hit me. Is this how they see me?

The one with the buzzcut passed me the joint.

"I'll pass." I'd already told her that when we got there. I no longer wished I were sixteen again. I didn't know that smoke, plain old smoke, could get you this buzzed, even with all the windows open.

"Mama!" Mar jutted her head out of the white scarf that fastened her to David. "Now me!" she lifted her bare, chubby arms.

I nodded to let her know it was okay, and she kept talking, her eyes glued to me, while everyone else kept smoking and drinking like nothing was up.

"The most intense experience of my life was when you and Papa died because of me."

"No, baby girl. No."

"What do you mean? Papa's dead and you'll be gone soon."

"No, Mar. I'm a widow, but you'll have a father. I married a child, and now I'm trying to come back to life because I want to be with a man. I'm not abandoning you."

"You're not?"

"I'm not, really."

"Oh." And then she tucked her arms back in the scarf and let her head drop as she went back to sleep.

So long as Mar keeps asking—asking for milk, for my arms—everything's fine. So long as she understands that I'm the one who holds her and that she doesn't hold me. So long as she understands that she doesn't have to make me smile, or smile to make me happy.

I only have one arm and she keeps asking for it. I only have one breast and she keeps asking for it. You can stay dead, rest peacefully. No need to rush back—I'm not ready yet.

In these eight-almost-nine months since our baby's birth, I've been tempted to drop chin to chest, press my forehead against hers and say *ai*, baby, *ai*. To let myself fall on her. To ask her for milk without even realizing it. I have no memories of my eight-almost-nine months but could swear that when I was on the other side of the looking glass, I learned to live backward.

So long as Mar keeps asking, everything's fine.

I asked Lali to come but she's taking a while. Today, for the first time, I've noticed her colossal breasts. I think about *Amarcord*, about Fellini, about drowning between her two tits, but I don't really want that anymore. Am I getting better?

David starts making the coffee and she takes a seat in one of the red chairs, letting him handle it.

"I came to visit because of your note, but now I see you've got this clever young man who's already helping out with the clothes and the diapers and everything, huh?" She winks at David, who's up and humming as he screws the top of the moka pot closed, then she swats him on the butt and chuckles. Her white roots have grown out, gaining ground over the dye's reddish orange. She can't seem to wrap her head around it all. She looks at me: "So you just hang about like that now? You don't even cover your breast? Want me to knit you half a bra? I've got some yellow yarn—it's summery."

I'm sitting in the high chair, holding Mar with one arm. She's breastfeeding from the table. I laugh and shake my head:

"I plan to be all better by the time summer comes around. You can make me a full bikini if you want. How about that?"

"Sure." She pulls out an empty, blue ballpoint pen from her apron pocket and jots it down, a ghost note. "What's that sound?"

That's my laptop, but I thought only I could hear it. David turns around once he's done lighting the fire and faces Lali:

"Her husband, who calls her on Skype all day long, on the computer, you know? But she ignores him. She won't pick up."

"But isn't . . . didn't her husband die?" She asks, lips pursed, averting her eyes. "And there's a Wifi signal here?"

I'm stunned. All of a sudden, Mar peels away from my nipple and frowns at me. I thought Roger's Skype calls were only in my frazzled head, in my chiclet keyboard, in this concoction passing as a novel. I thought they were just part of the narrative I'd fabricated about our split.

David and Lali don't seem the least bit alarmed at this discovery. They contemplate my unhinged episodes like one would stare at an abstract painting, eyes squinted, dismissing any hint at meaning with a wave of the hand. Mar's gaze, like the finest catheter, almost like a pliant needle, pierces the corner of my eye and exits through my heart, bum-bum, bum-bum.

At the other end of the oilcloth, what remains of the star scoots around—moist, with just two legs, one of them faded. She shuffles over to me, and Lali bursts with laughter, spitting and banging on the wood with her hands. I leave Mar on the table and she balances on her arms and feet; she can only crawl backward.

The day you and I spent in town, we ended up drinking some crisp, white wine and snacking on potato chips out on the terrace at Bar dels Pescadors. I sat the baby on my lap and let her have a dried peach, which she gnawed on with delight. Everything went right for you that day.

You asked, Can I tell you about me? Fuck, why are you asking my permission, I replied. Because you're always getting tired of me. I'll complain once I get tired. Go ahead, I said, handing over the reins. So I want to tell you about the three worst versions of myself. I rolled my eyes up toward the sky, just for a couple seconds, poking fun. You counted with your fingers: One, the Condescending me, who tells me I do everything right and cradles me and keeps me from facing any-and-all fuckups; two, the Disconcerted me, who brushes me aside whenever I need to face any challenge that demands my full attention, You're a little kid, he tells me, Stick your head inside this hole and don't fix it. And three, the Perfectionist, who wants to control everything, and if anything I do isn't impeccable, he won't even let me roll up my sleeves and get to work. To sum up: You're not worth shit, you don't deserve it, no, no, and no. It's awful, Muri. So look, you concluded, opening up your arms, I've got love for all three. They were useful to me at some point in my life, but now they're stopping me from evolving and becoming a man, so I've got to leave them here. And you dusted off your hands.

I smiled, we raised our glasses, and then I took your picture—the first one that I had printed out, the one I glued your Playmobil cowboy hat to.

Then I begged you to leave the three of you anywhere but here, Please, leave them somewhere else because I want my next novel to take place here, on the beach, at the hotel or at one of the *casetes*, you know? You looked at me to say, Now you're telling me what to do again, let me do as I fucking please, so I don't know where you ended up leaving them. If it was here, then I think your three musketeers must have drowned in the ocean, because I haven't seen them around. All the characters I've ever written about have come from me and my own idiosyncrasies. Your three saboteurs have left without a trace, D'Artagnan.

So, you said, And you? Do you ever self-sabotage? I'd already had more than a few sips of wine so I entered the ring and let loose: My main and probably only voice is Distrust in your abilities, baby, in your ability to change. You looked at me like you were about to get up and go, like after you'd laid yourself bare, my distrust felt even more harsh, but I went on. It feeds off of my fear of being with a real man, feeds off my fear of loss. But of losing what?, you asked. You, silly, of losing the one I love. I think anyone who's man enough, a person enough, adult enough, will see that I'm a fake and abandon me before even scratching past the surface. You picked up a potato chip and stuck it between my lips. I said: I hereby decide not to be your mother, nor anyone else's. Mar turned around, looked up to me, and I assured her, Yes, I will be yours. We laughed and I fixed her hat—it'd gotten lopsided with her gesture and wasn't blocking the sun. I hereby decide to live with my fear of living with a man and of possibly being abandoned. I hereby decide to live with the energy that this fear stirs up in me. I hereby decide to live with uncertainty and silence and to apply this principle to the rest of my relations. Damn, you said.

I opened my mouth and took the potato chip— the one you were still pinching between your fingers—in holy communion, and while I chewed I bit down hard on my tongue and said, Look, I bit my tongue. I stuck my tongue out to show you the wound and you said, Good thing tongues heal so fast.

I don't know how long I have left, if I'll survive, if I'll be mutilated forever. I thought this was all about rebirth, but now I'm not so sure. When I-my-husband's-mother dies, I don't know if there'll be anything left of me. Maybe just one tit—no regeneration in sight.

I hop with my arm until I reach the starfish's bucket, which is usually in the bathroom. My head's getting very heavy and my bicep's hyperatrophied. I carry the star in my teeth and drop her in the water. I lean my head in, see myself reflected, beg the star to offer some answers, but she has none.

Why am I losing pieces if not to regenerate myself wholly? If I was just supposed to disappear— disappear completely—then why not write that I was dying and got cremated and call it a day? Why the starfish? Why the *casetes*? Why a parenthesis? Where am I going?

My husband died in one piece. He disappeared on the highway in the car he'd borrowed from the shop, since ours had a leak. Now I have to be reborn from the ashes. Did he give them to me, or did I steal them from him? What was there to burn?

"What are you looking for, *guapa*?" David walks into the room and leans on the arch separating the two rooms while I rummage around the closet.

"My husband's ashes, his writings. I put them here, I think."

"What?"

"Before I came here." I stick my head inside the armoire. "He burned everything he'd written, and I stole the ashes so he wouldn't be tempted to eat them. I'm certain he's writing from somewhere else now."

"You mean from heaven?"

"Did Lali leave?"

"No. She's playing with Mar on the staircase. They're singing the vowels already."

"Found them."

A few minutes later, we're in front of the closed restaurant that juts out from the beach's southernmost tip, among the ramps and cement steps, above the rocks, at the lower end of my left parenthesis. From a white and blue balcony, I prepare for my goodbye ritual, like in the movies. Mar claps her hands in Lali's arms. David carries me as I stir the ashes with my hand; he's holding the jar for me, too.

I let my hand open and close, open and close. Mar follows suit. The raging sea eats up the charred, motley letters my husband wrote in life, thrashing them against the rocks. I do what Max Brod didn't do for Franz Kafka and the fish come and eat up the late childhood he'd siphoned through the ink of his pens.

"I know you're still writing somewhere," I call out against the wind.

I think about how I'm hoping that he writes differently now, but don't say it out loud. The scene feels good enough as is.

The starfish has gotten comfortable in my hair. She looks good on me. Her two arms form a headband, a red-orange one. She knows we don't have much time left and wants to spend it all with me. I won't say no. I'm about to lose my head—literally, not like when you say, honey, you're making me lose my head. David knows that my head'll fall off but doesn't say anything. He sings to himself as he sweeps, *lerelereleree* . . . Mar knows it but she doesn't know how to talk and eyes the starfish's only arms as she coos: aaa, eee, iii . . . She wants to touch the star with her finger but the starfish shrinks back. I write in bed and our daughter lets out little shrieks as she licks and gnaws on her stuffed Nemo, who can't find his father.

I'll send you everything I've written soon. Read it if you've got the time.

Mar's turning nine months old in two days and still isn't crawling. She scoots backward, as you've seen, but doesn't do a normal, forward crawl.

Did you know I never crawled? I went straight from sitting to walking. I spent a year and a half turning it over in my head, studying, but once I stood up and took my first step, I never fell once. Never. I'm sure you're not surprised, since this is me we're talking about.

I want Mar to crawl, to try things, recoil, dare, roll around, to be like you. To make a lot of mistakes. But without all your frustration. To laugh.

This is where her exterogestation ends, a second birth. But I don't plan on going all that far, even if I'm ultimately reduced to a single nipple.

This is where my mothering of you ends, too. I don't ever want to give birth to you, and we need to get that through our heads. Thanks for dying beforehand and making it easier for me to switch gears.

I'm five fingers, one arm, a leaking breast, and a dried-out heart. Writer, mother who holds, mother who feeds, mother and bride who loves. I have no sex, I don't eat, don't scoot, don't see myself, don't smell, don't speak.

I woke up from my nap today, alone under the *caseta*, among the columns, and my head had turned to dry sand. The sea spoke to me and I abandoned the search for my right parenthesis, mostly because I'm obviously handicapped. When I write "alone," I mean with Mar. The hardest thing about writing all this is constantly asking myself, scene after scene, what's Mar doing, where is she, how is she? To live as a mother is to tell stories in that way, with an appendage character.

David touches me so I know he's there and helps me hold my baby, improvising; I wouldn't be able to give him instructions except in writing, on screen, but I act like I haven't thought of that and leave him be. I notice Mar's sucking, hold her as tight as I can, and write, write, write. My writing hand. Blindly.

There's not much left.

The one arm the starfish has left curls into a bracelet for me and I make no effort to peel her away or leave her in the bucket. She struggles to breathe but this is what she wants, and I respect that. I don't know if she's a mother or a daughter to me, but she needs me and I have pity. Pi-ty. I write "pity." Then I know: she's a mother. I'm sure of it. The star shows me how to resurrect even though she's never before done it herself. She shows me, leaving pieces of life along the way.

I don't know where I am. I can sense the flurry like the closeness of windows. Or maybe I'm on the patio. I entrust everything I am to David and don't control him, boss him around, or ask for anything. I only write and try to survive. I learn.

I'm grateful to Mar for the time she's gifted me, no bells or whistles. She knows I'll come out a better mother and doesn't cry or ask for anything. She just waits.

I'm five fingers, one arm, a leaking breast, and a dried-out heart, but I think I'm lucky.

The whole time I've been here you've been so busy calling and calling that you've skipped right past the fact that I don't have internet I don't turn my phone on I don't have eyes or ears or a mouth. You skip right past the technological barriers and barge into my mutilated life. You're pigheaded, and I'm scared.

What do you really expect from an arm that drags a breast along behind it? I don't have a head. I-don't-have-a-head. I once had the hardest head on the planet but it crumbled in the wind.

Today an email arrived through the virtual waves of your stubbornness and, since I can't read it, can't hear it, David helped me decipher the words: he laid me on the table, opened the chest of drawers, took out my letters, and arranged them—placing them down and picking them up, placing them down and picking them up—on the oilcloth. That way, I could read what you had sent me with just the touch of my fingertips.

To my dear wife, Muriel, how annoying you are.

There are things I want to say to you that you won't let me say. I don't want to make a big deal out of it but you shouldn't have closed yourself off like that. You talked about taking a break, a parenthesis, but that's gone on long enough.

Don't think that just because you left I've gotten complacent.

Things keep changing. That old me's no longer around, he died in that car, he went up in flames with that writing, but now you've got me, a new man, with just the right measure of child and all that that entails. I'm not angry anymore.

I'm getting really tired of being apart and I'm sticking to my challenge: the silence you've asked of me. Every day I walk by our beach and wet my feet in the waves. They no longer make me shrink back. I walk, and they wet my feet and change me, coming and going, from left to right, over and over again, while I keep walking, and they speak of your silence, and of mine, and they say that to speak less you have to think less, a lot less. Those waves are my thoughts, and they come, but they also go.

Now I live in a constant state of magical silence, I weigh less, I move softly, and I want to fall into you as I hold you up.

When the time's right for you, I'll rise from the ashes, like a phoenix, to support you as you do the same, and to once again find the right path for our bodies to converse while our minds keep quiet.

P.S. I just finished writing my novel.

I'm guessing it's nighttime. I guess I was sleeping, if a body like mine can sleep. I guess I was lying on the bed and I thought I noticed my daughter's warm, sleeping body and David's body sprawled at my side, when suddenly, a slow, undeniable force tugged at my wrist and pulled me off the mattress, dragged me across the floor and down the stairs in fits and starts, and, once on the sand, continued to drag me to the water, little by little, cold and silent.

Then we plunged in, the star and I, her body a bracelet around my wrist.

Then what had to happen *did* happen, except for one thing, an unimportant detail that appealed to my hunger for perfection, shook me and said:

"Hey, it doesn't end here."

The both of us, our hands clasped, entered the night sea, the dark waters where you can't see a thing and think only of pitch-black sharks. We began to grow, each cell regenerating, sweetly and slowly. It didn't hurt. It tickled. It tickled and burned a bit, from the salt. My body was taking shape, bit by bit, like a predictable epilogue, and I wondered if what was happening to me could be christened as a right parenthesis, but no, I ruled that out almost instantly. It doesn't end here.

My left breast emerged from my sternum, round and full of milk, unhurriedly, and then my arm, and my head, my hair much longer than before, then slowly the lung I was missing, my diaphragm, my empty intestines, and everything else, my waist, vagina, and legs. All there.

I put my hand on my labia and parted them as you part a fish you're about to stuff, and with my new fingertip, I traced the old birthing scar. I had hoped that my new body wouldn't be sewn up, that my labia would be brand new, intact, but they aren't

at all. The scar's still there, with every stitch, minus the pain and stinging, but with all of the same fears. Those from before giving birth and those from after. All of them. It must be that my star, who loves me so, thought it better for my new body to remember the wound.

When I wrote "except for one thing," I meant my heart.

I stood; naked, wet, salty, upright in the water, which came up to my thighs. My star, now whole, was latched to the center of my stomach and pecking at me. I glanced down at myself, checked every part with my hands, and my heart was hanging outside of my body. My new body had only accepted my old heart as a pumping machine. As if to command:

"Keep going, but don't you come inside."

"Bum-bum, bum-bum." Poor thing.

My star slid to my legs, taking her time, kissed my left knee and left ankle, and finally came down to the sand and, walking across the seabed, parted from me ever so slowly. I know I won't see her again.

When we had just started out, when we didn't know who we were, when you didn't have a home, when I didn't have your hourglass, only a digital clock, the neighbors would bang on our walls because we would make love all night long.

We would take photos of ourselves naked, we'd

shower with the cassette stereo on, we smelled like sex.

Six years have passed.

We have a car, kakebo, literary projects, contracts, and a daughter. We've gotten a taste of tantra and other exotic dishes and we know that the horizon is more than a line.

It all tastes like honey, feels like honey, when you're just starting out.

I want to live in a cascade of left parentheses but with you, always with you. I know you want it, too, and that it's possible.

((((((((((. . .

Ver-ti-go.

I get out of the water. Salt and doubt trickle off me and I cry. It's pitch black out and the sea quiets down.

I see David coming out of the *caseta*, with his tracksuit bottoms on, a backpack, and the baby in his arms. He drops his bag in front of the door, comes down to the sandy part of the beach, lays out a sarong underneath the *caseta*, between the columns, and sets Mar down on it. She claps in her diaper . . . . He waves goodbye to me, grabs his backpack, calmly climbs the stairs, and vanishes from my sight forever, and afterward I hear his blue van's engine as he drives off.

I turn and look at the lower part of my left parenthesis: the large rocks where, in front of the restaurant, the waves break; the rocks where I let my husband's ashes take flight.

The first thing I see is a wet hand, his fingers long and dexterous, peaking over the rounded top of a rock. He rises bit by bit, and from behind the rock appear his dark, brooding eyes, his half-smile, and his asymmetrical chest. My heart, hanging out of my chest, is beating hard.

I look at Mar for a moment: she's already on her way, crawling and laughing, looking for her dad.

And he—naked, with his perfect legs and limp penis—is already walking toward me. I'm dying for him to turn so I can see his ass, but I wait. I'm embarrassed and I fight to hold his gaze, to keep my throat from closing. He advances, he's enormous, a firm column, feet with roots.

He stands before me and doesn't say a thing, he keeps still. His black hair drips sea on his shoulders. He looks at my heart. He holds it in his hands, lovingly so, and cradles it. Sings to it. Ever so carefully, and asking permission with his eyes, he puts it back into my chest, which accepts and heals it.

Then we let our bodies talk while we keep quiet for a while.

Mar's fallen asleep at our side and the sun rises.

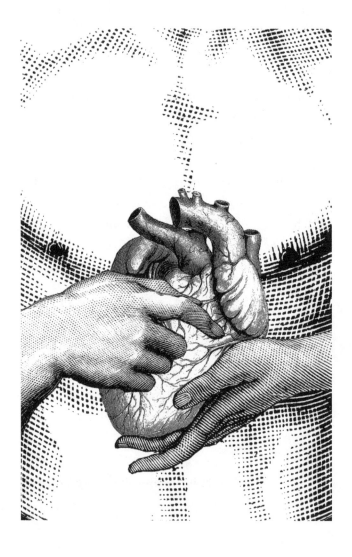

I began writing to close a parenthesis, to escape a widowhood that had its knife at my throat, and to mourn as if drowning in an evaporated puddle.

Casetes Beach served as an opening parenthesis, a left parenthesis, a backdrop for the credits.

I've tried everything: fiction, metaphor, therapy, and reality, too. And that parenthesis won't close.

Out there on the beach, an immense and infinite sea carries me out to a horizon that doesn't exist, that I cannot touch no matter how far I swim. My parenthesis holds water, that's it, that's how I came to choose it, and now it treats me as it likes, fluctuating, mercurial, ineffable, unyielding.

Life by your side, a left parenthesis without a right. A small and open text that explains a longer—and perhaps more important—one that we no longer require.

Thanks to the following people—in order of appearance—for helping make this book possible: Roger Coch, Leticia Asenjo, Ramon Mas, Ricard Planas, Aitana Carrasco, and Maria Cabrera.

MEGAN BERKOBIEN is an educator, translator, and organizer. She holds a PhD in comparative literature from the University of Michigan and is the founder of the Emergent Translators Collective. She is a worker-owner at the Red Emma's Collective, a radical bookstore, cafe, free school, and community events space in Baltimore.

MARÍA CRISTINA HALL is a Mexican-American writer and translator. She studied creative writing at Columbia University and translation studies at Universitat Pompeu Fabra in Barcelona. She now lives in Mexico City, where she's doing a PhD on return migration at UNAM. She wrote the chapbook *Sueños de la Malaria* (Herring Publishers) and recently translated *The Dead Won't Die Here* (Editorial Argonáutica). Her first book, *Fantasía Fértil* (Medusa Books), is now available in Spain. She and Megan Berkobien edited *Absinthe*, an anthology of contemporary women's writing in Catalan (U. of Michigan).

OPEN LETTER

OPEN LETTER

OPEN LETTER

9 781948 830522